Dragons

Illustrated by Peter Scott

Written by Judy Tatchell

Designed by Reuben Barrance

Digital imaging by Keith Furnival

Flying dragons

For hundreds of years, all over the world, people have been telling stories about dragons. Many of the dragons were big, scaly, flying creatures like these.

In some tales, the dragons swooped and soared over land and sea, looking down on golden castles, green fields and dark forests below.

Oh no!

The dragons came down to land when they felt hungry or sleepy. But some dragons came down to make mischief, too.

In a dragon's den

There are lots of stories about dragons who loved gold, silver and jewels. They hid their treasure in secret caves.

I can see you!

People said that these dragons slept with one eye open, so nobody could creep past and steal anything.

The dragons often curled themselves around their treasure to keep it safe.

Anyone who touched even the smallest coin was in BIG trouble.

In some tales, people tricked the dragons and stole their treasure...

Fire and frost

The scariest tales are about dragons that breathed fire.

It was said that one fiery blast from a dragon's mouth could turn a castle to ash or burn down a whole forest.

Other stories tell of frost dragons that blew an icy cold wind, which froze everything solid.

Their frost looked so pretty, it glittered and glistened...

Lovely sparkles!

Baby dragons

Some stories tell how dragons laid eggs, like birds do.

If an egg got cold, the baby would die. So the mother breathed her hot flames over it.

The stories say that after a few meals baby dragons were strong enough to fly. They could even breathe fire...

EEK! Don't huff and puff at me!

Chinese dragons

In China, people tell tales of friendly dragons who helped people and brought good luck.

This dragon could bring good weather and make the wind blow.

Hmm. Who can I help today?

We need wind in our sails.

In Chinese stories, the dragons had horns like a stag, a flowing mane like a lion and long, wavy feelers.

Their snaky bodies were covered with fishlike scales. Their feet had five toes with claws on them.

She-dragons often carried beautiful fans.

Chinese dragons didn't have wings. The stories say they flew by pure magic.

Welsh dragons

Wales is a land of misty mountains and tumbling streams. There are many tales about dragons in Wales.

This dragon guarded a well full of cold, clear water.

Other dragons lived in secret places.

For hundreds of years, there has been a red dragon on the Welsh flag. The story of that dragon is told below.

The Dragon of Wales

Flying serpents

Stories from South America tell of snaky dragons called flying serpents. Like snakes, they had no legs.

The dragons were very wise. It is said that they knew almost all the secrets in the world.

Some, like these, had long, glittering feathers as well as scales.

Shall I tell you a secret?

On the ground, the dragons slithered like snakes. They curled up to rest.

But first, you had to get hold of some teeth...

Most people believe that dragons, like giants
and fairies, only live in stories. But who
knows? Maybe once, in a faraway time,
dragons, or creatures like them, really
did fly and crawl over the earth...

Edited by Kirsteen Rogers

First published in 2005 by Usborne Publishing Ltd, Usborne House,
83-85 Saffron Hill, London EC1N 8RT, England.
www.usborne.com
Copyright © Usborne Publishing Ltd, 2005.

Printed in China.